When CARROT Met COOKIE

To Kenna Kay (a.k.a. Auntie K.K.),
who always has my back. YDB!—ESP

For Pendy, Coco, and Flo, my veggie-loving sweeties!—JF

PENGUIN WORKSHOP
An Imprint of Penguin Random House LLC, New York

Text copyright © 2021 by Erica S. Perl. Illustrations copyright © 2021 by Jonathan Fenske.
All rights reserved. Published simultaneously in hardcover and paperback by Penguin Workshop, an imprint of Penguin Random House LLC, New York. PENGUIN and PENGUIN WORKSHOP are trademarks of Penguin Books Ltd, and the W colophon is a registered trademark of Penguin Random House LLC.
Manufactured in China.

Visit us online at www.penguinrandomhouse.com.

Library of Congress Control Number: 2021006858

ISBN 9780593226322 (pbk)   10 9 8 7 6 5 4 3 2 1

When
CARROT
Met
COOKIE

by Erica S. Perl
illustrated by Jonathan Fenske

Penguin Workshop

From the moment they met,
Carrot liked Cookie.

And Cookie liked Carrot.

Carrot was bright, grounded,
and great at rooting for friends.

Cookie was sweet, warm, and cheerfully chipper.

Carrot taught Cookie to dip.

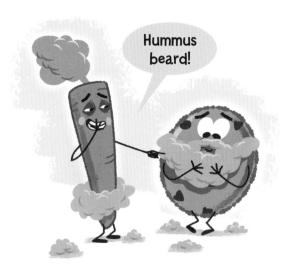

Hummus beard!

Cookie taught Carrot to dunk.

They were the best of friends.

Cookie had other friends, like Cupcake and Lollipop.
They were sweet . . . most of the time.

But when Cookie didn't speak up, Carrot wilted.

So, the next time Cookie was in the mood for a dunk, Carrot said,

I'll pass.

Carrot had other friends, too, like Cuke and Zuke.
They were cool . . . most of the time.

But when Carrot didn't speak up, Cookie felt crummy.

So, the next time Carrot asked Cookie to go for a dip, Cookie said,

No, thanks.

One day, Cookie's mom asked, "How's Carrot?"
"I don't know," admitted Cookie. "I guess we're not
really friends anymore."

"Good!" said Cookie's grandpa. "Back in my day,
desserts acted like desserts."

Cookie's mom took Cookie aside.
"Some of Grandpa's ideas are a little stale," she said.
"I think you should go talk to your aunt C.C."

"Hi, Cookie!" said Cookie's aunt. "Where's Carrot?"
Cookie crumbled.
Then Cookie told Aunt C.C. everything.

"I'm so confused," added Cookie. "Just because I'm a dessert and Carrot's a vegetable doesn't mean we can't be friends, does it?"

"Not at all." Aunt C.C. pulled out a photo album. "Have I ever told you about my parents?"

Cookie went to talk to Carrot.

When Cookie got to the part
about Cuke and Zuke,
Carrot turned beet red.

"I should have said something," said Carrot. "Next time, I will."

"Me too," promised Cookie, thinking about Cupcake and Lollipop.

"Want to come for a dip?" asked Carrot. "Cuke invited everyone over."

Cookie thought about Grandpa.
Cookie thought about Cuke and Zuke.

But then, Cookie had an idea.

"Did Cuke really say *everyone*?" Cookie asked.

"This party is pretty sweet," said Cupcake. "I'll say," said Cuke. "Cookie, you and your friends are cool. Thanks for coming."

Cookie smiled. "Anytime. You ready, Carrot?
One ... two ... three ..."